To: St Nicks YMCA

From: Miss Regan

:)

We will forever be thankful to the Valentine Davies family
for allowing us to share his work with the world.

Text of *Miracle on 34th Street* novella © 1947 by Valentine Davies Estate
Cover and internal design and illustrations © 2018 by Sourcebooks, Inc.
Illustrations by James Newman Gray
Text adapted for picture book by Susanna Leonard Hill
Text copyright © 2018 by Valentine Davies Estate

Sourcebooks and the colophon are registered trademarks of Sourcebooks, Inc.

Published by Sourcebooks Jabberwocky, an imprint of Sourcebooks, Inc.
P.O. Box 4410, Naperville, Illinois 60567–4410
(630) 961-3900
Fax: (630) 961-2168
sourcebooks.com

Library of Congress Cataloging-in-Publication Data is on file with the publisher.

Source of Production: Shenzhen Wing King Tong Paper Products Co. Ltd., Shenzhen, Guangdong Province, China
Date of Production: June 2018
Run Number: 5012562

Printed and bound in China.

WKT 10 9 8 7 6 5 4 3 2 1

Miracle
on 34th Street

A Storybook Edition of the Christmas Classic

by Valentine Davies

pictures by James Newman Gray

adapted for picture book by Susanna Leonard Hill

sourcebooks
jabberwocky

Floats stretched like a rainbow along Central Park West.

Huge balloons tugged at their ropes as if to say, come on! Let's go!

Tubas *oompahed* and a bass drum *boomed* as the marching band tuned up.

The Macy's Thanksgiving Day Parade was about to start.

"Look, Mother!" Susan exclaimed. She pointed to Santa's sleigh at the end of the line. Santa was snoring!

"Oh, no!" said Mother. "The parade will start any minute and Santa is the most important part. He's the grand finale!"

Mother was in charge of the whole Macy's Thanksgiving Day Parade. She spent much of the year getting everything ready so the parade would run just right. But now, moments before the start, Santa was sound asleep in the back of the sleigh! She needed to fix this before the grumpy Mr. Sawyer found out and complained to Mr. Macy.

"Excuse me, ma'am," said an elderly bearded gentleman. "May I be of some help?"

Mother took one look at the man and smiled. He was small and round with a bushy, white beard, rosy cheeks, and eyes that twinkled with merriment. He was perfect!

Quick as a wink, she helped him into a Santa costume and onto the float.

"What a wonderful Santa he is," Mother marveled. "The best we've ever had! I'm going to invite him to dinner tonight to say thank you."

That night, Mother and Susan, their kind neighbor Fred, and the old
gentleman gathered around the table for Thanksgiving Dinner.

Susan couldn't help but ask, "Who are you, sir? And how did you
know to help my mother at just the right time?"

"Why, I'm Kris Kringle, my dear," the old gentleman said with a wink. "I knew to help because I am, indeed, Santa Claus!"

Susan crossed her arms. "I don't believe you. Mother says there's no such thing as Santa Claus, or any of the other silly things children are told in make-believe."

Kris looked surprised. "No Santa Claus?" he asked. "No make-believe? Surely you've read fairy-tales, or played house, or zoo?"

Susan shrugged. "No, that's not for me," she said. "Mother doesn't believe in any of those things so I don't either."

Kris replied, "But, my dear! Make-believe and pretending are what being a child is all about! It's about imagination. How would you like to make snowballs in the summertime? How would you like to visit the Statue of Liberty in the morning and in the afternoon fly south with a flock of geese?"

Susan thought it would be amazing to have such adventures.

"Come," said Kris. He led her to the living room. "I'll teach you to pretend."

In no time, Kris and Susan were a couple of monkeys swinging through the jungle. Susan had never had so much fun.

"What would you like for Christmas?" Kris asked, in between monkey noises.

"Nothing," said Susan.

"Come now," Kris smiled kindly. "There must be something."

"Well…" Susan hesitated. "There is one thing." Her voice grew quiet. "I wish we could have a little house in the country with a swing in the backyard. Me, and Mother, and, well…" She glanced sideways to the dining room where Mother laughed with Fred. "A family," she whispered. She showed Kris a picture she'd saved. "This house," she said, feeling silly.

"That's a tall order, young lady," Kris said.

"If you can't do it," said Susan, "I'll know you're not really Santa, just a nice old man with a white beard like mother says."

"I'll do my best," Kris promised. "But just because every child can't get her wish doesn't mean there's no Santa Claus. Sometimes children wish for things that aren't right for them. Just as I'll try, I want you to try to believe Santa is real."

Susan smiled. Just then, Mother and Fred joined them.

"You did such a good job today," said Mother to Kris. "Mr. Macy would be thrilled if you'd stay on to work as Santa until Christmas."

"I've got room next door if you need a place to stay," offered Fred. "I'd love to have the real Santa Claus stay with me!" he said as he winked at Susan.

"Don't make silly statements like that to her, Fred," whispered Mother.

"Have some faith!" Fred replied. "You've just got too much common sense. Faith is believing in things when common sense tells you not to."

Kris beamed. "Looks like it's all settled then," he said. "I thank you for your kindness."

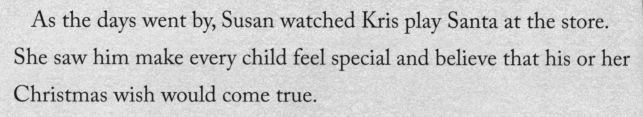

As the days went by, Susan watched Kris play Santa at the store. She saw him make every child feel special and believe that his or her Christmas wish would come true.

Susan heard him talk to children in different languages when they didn't speak English. He even signed to a child who was deaf. Their faces lit up with delight at being understood.

"How can he know how to speak to everyone?" Susan asked her mother. He was truly jolly and kind. Susan knew his beard was real— she had tugged on it herself. "He must be Santa!"

"Darling, that doesn't make him Santa Claus," Mother said. "I speak French, but that doesn't make me French toast!"

But even Mother was beginning to wonder...

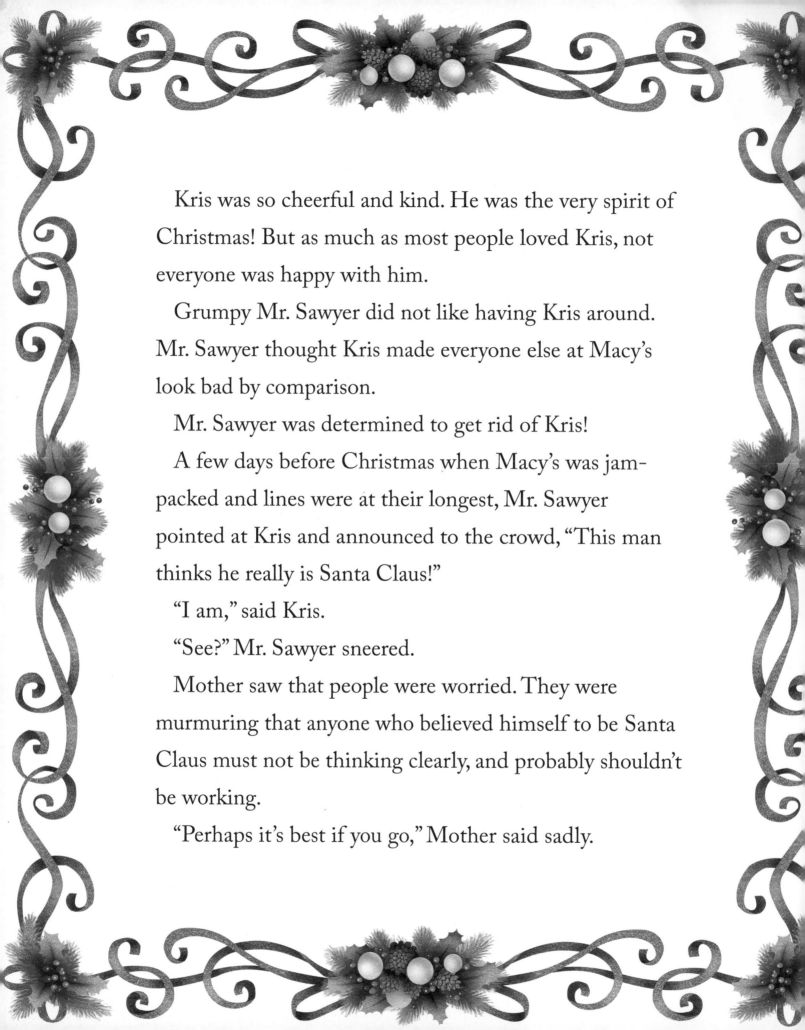

Kris was so cheerful and kind. He was the very spirit of Christmas! But as much as most people loved Kris, not everyone was happy with him.

Grumpy Mr. Sawyer did not like having Kris around. Mr. Sawyer thought Kris made everyone else at Macy's look bad by comparison.

Mr. Sawyer was determined to get rid of Kris!

A few days before Christmas when Macy's was jam-packed and lines were at their longest, Mr. Sawyer pointed at Kris and announced to the crowd, "This man thinks he really is Santa Claus!"

"I am," said Kris.

"See?" Mr. Sawyer sneered.

Mother saw that people were worried. They were murmuring that anyone who believed himself to be Santa Claus must not be thinking clearly, and probably shouldn't be working.

"Perhaps it's best if you go," Mother said sadly.

"Goodbye," Mr. Sawyer said triumphantly. "Have a nice trip back to the North Pole!"

Kris left Macy's sadly. Why did no one believe?

Fred, Susan, and Mother followed Kris outside.

"You can't let them treat you this way," said Fred. "We must go to court—I'll represent you and prove that you are indeed Santa! If we win, everyone will know you're the real Santa."

"But if we lose," Fred continued, "you will lose more than your job. You may ruin your good name and children will stop believing in you!"

Kris was nervous, but he believed in Fred. He hoped everything would be okay.

Susan was nervous, too. She liked Kris and didn't want anyone to make fun of him or cause him trouble.

The following week in court, Fred called his first witness.

It was the prosecutor's son!

"Do you believe Santa is real?" Fred asked the boy.

"Yes!" said the boy. "My daddy told me Santa is real and he would never tell me something that isn't so…would you, Daddy?" The boy looked right at his father.

"Of course Santa is real!" cried the prosecutor, Mr. Mara. He did not want his son to think he told lies.

Fred patted Kris on the back. Mr. Mara had just admitted that Santa was real! "We won!" he whispered.

Once the young boy left the courtroom, Mr. Mara said, "BUT there is no proof that THIS MAN is Santa Claus!"

"He's right," said the judge, looking at Fred. "The State of New York is willing to agree that Santa is real, but that doesn't mean Mr. Kringle is him."

Fred glanced worriedly at Kris. How on Earth could he prove that Kris was the one and only Santa?

"You have until tomorrow," announced the judge. "We'll look forward to seeing your proof."

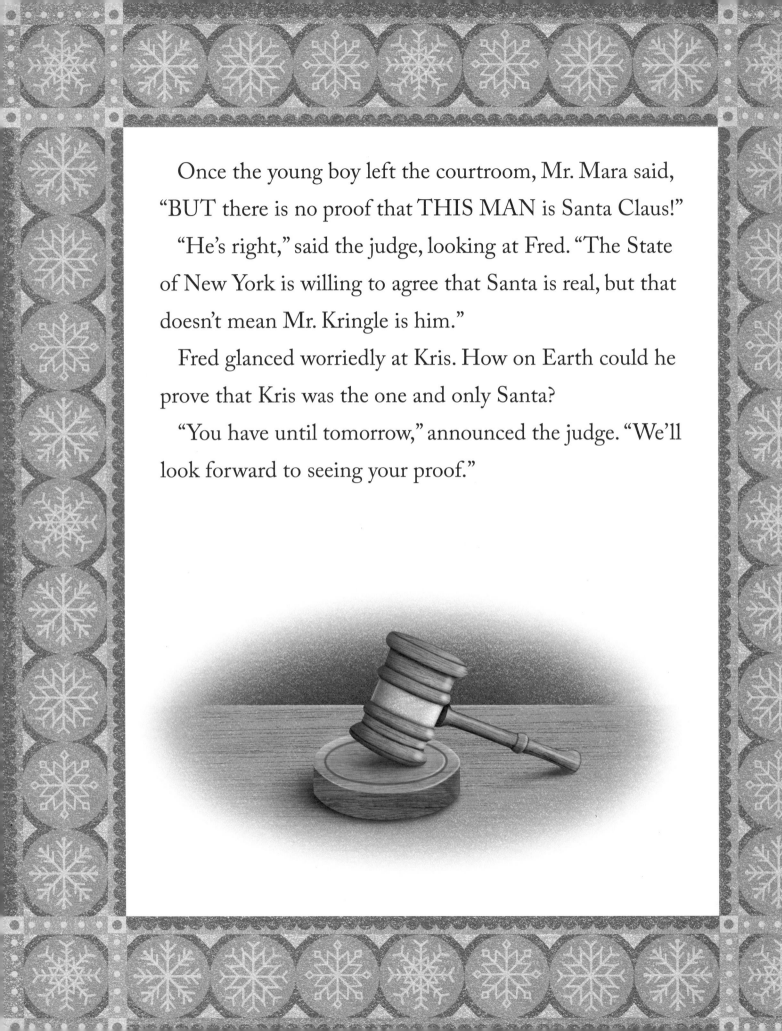

The next morning, everyone arrived at the courthouse. Mother and Susan were sitting in the courtroom to show support for Fred and Kris, hoping for a miracle that would help them both.

The judge entered the courtroom and began the trial. He asked Fred, "Well, where's your proof?"

Fred was quiet. He didn't have any proof. He was up all night and could not think of an answer to this problem.

Just then, one of the courtroom doormen came forward and whispered in Fred's ear.

Fred's eyes widened. Then he smiled. He gestured toward the door and called out, "Bring them in!"

"Your Honor," Fred said to the judge, "here is our proof!"
One postal worker after another paraded into the courtroom loaded down with bags of mail.

They emptied each bag on the judge's desk until it was covered in letters.

Every single one was addressed to Santa! The postmen had read about the case in the papers and realized it was much faster to reach Santa in New York than to send the letters to the North Pole!

"The United States Post Office is an official government agency," said Fred. "It's against the law for them to deliver mail to the wrong person. If they say Kris is Santa, he is!"

In the face of such overwhelming love and support, no further proof was needed.

"Case closed!" said the judge. "Merry Christmas, everyone!"

Kris had a celebration on Christmas Day and invited Susan, Mother, and Fred to come over for the fun and presents.

Susan looked and looked but she did not find her Christmas wish under the tree. Hadn't they proven that Kris was really Santa?

Mother tried to reassure Susan by saying, "Just because things didn't turn out the way you wanted, you still have to believe in people."

As Mother, Fred, and Susan were driving home after the celebration, Susan wanted to be happy. The judge had said Kris was the real Santa. But if that was so, why hadn't she gotten her Christmas wish?

Susan wanted to trust what Mother had said. She began to whisper, "I believe" over and over. Just then she saw the house of her dreams—the exact one she had shown Kris!

"Stop!" she cried. "Stop the car!"

The moment the car pulled to a stop, Susan raced into the house with Mother and Fred on her heels.

Her bedroom was just as she'd imagined.

And the back yard…

and the tree…

…even the swing!

Susan turned and saw Mother with Fred's arm around her. Every part of her wish was coming true. "He really is Santa," she said, eyes shining. "He really is!"

The End